My Brother the Gross Out

by Michael J. Pellowski

illustrated by Ann Iosa

To my son,
Martin

Published by Willowisp Press, Inc.
401 E. Wilson Bridge Road, Worthington, Ohio 43085

Printed in the United States of America

10 9 8 7 6 5 4 3 2 1

ISBN 0-87406-476-7

One

"ICK! Stop spitting like that!" I yelled to my little brother, Gregory.

It was the first day of a new school year and Gregory the Gross Out was bugging me already.

"Can't you walk without spitting?" I asked him. "Do you have any idea how disgusting it is to watch somebody spit every five seconds?"

Gregory stopped. He looked at me and my friend, Jilly Duncan, and smiled in a devilish way. Then he spit into the street, making the loudest, ickiest sound he could.

"EEE-YUK!" groaned Jilly. "That kid is the grossest life form in the universe! What a way to start fifth grade, getting grossed out by a disgusting first grader." Jilly looked at me.

"Megan Evans," she said, "we're neighbors and best friends. We've walked to school together ever since kindergarten. But if you don't do something about your brother, you may have to walk to school alone from now on! I can't take it anymore."

Gregory just grinned and wiggled his finger. Slowly, he lifted his hand toward his face.

"Don't you dare!" I warned as I shook my fist in his direction. I knew what he was going to do—just to gross Jilly and me out.

"If you do I'll tell Dad," I said. "And Dad said if you picked your nose again he was going to throw out your dead bug collection."

"EEE-YUK!" shrieked Jilly again. "Megan, how did a nice girl like you ever get a brother like Gregory?" she muttered. "Spitting! Nose picking! Bug collecting! EEE-YUK!"

Sometimes I wondered myself how I got a brother like Gregory. Maybe an alien spaceship dropped him in the hospital and my parents brought him home by mistake. After all, we did look pretty different from each other.

Hardly anybody who saw us guessed that we were brother and sister.

"It's not my fault," I told Jilly. "I'd trade him in for a pet parakeet if I could, but I can't. And I can't walk to school without him, either. Mom said now that Gregory goes to school all day I have to walk him to and from school."

Jilly shook her head. "He's your brother...and I guess we're stuck with him."

"Stuck?" I muttered. "Hey! That gives me a good idea." I reached into my backpack and pulled out some bubble gum. "If he's chewing gum he can't spit," I whispered to Jilly.

"Good thinking," Jilly whispered back.

"Want some gum, Gregory?" I asked.

"Thanks," said Gregory. He snatched the whole pack from my hand.

"Hey!" I shouted. "I said *some* gum, not all of it."

"Forget it," Jilly whispered. "It's worth a whole pack of gum if he'll stop spitting."

We watched in horror as Gregory un-wrapped all the bubble gum pieces and stuffed them into his mouth. He began chomping on the big wad of gum like a cow. Jilly and I looked at each other and shook our heads.

"Here," Gregory said as he handed me back the empty gum package and wrappers.

My little brother may be gross, but at least he's not a litterbug. "Are you sure you've got enough in your mouth?" I asked him.

"Mmmpphhh," Gregory mumbled as he chewed the wad of gum. He kept his mouth open on purpose. The sound was revolting! Then he reached into his jacket pocket.

"Oh no! Not worms again!" Jilly groaned, slowly backing away. I got called down to the school office last year because Gregory came to kindergarten with live worms in his pockets.

"Phew," I sighed in relief when Gregory pulled out a chocolate bar instead of wiggling worms. But then, before our eyes, he unwrapped the candy and shoved it all into his mouth with the gum.

"Gag me!" said Jilly.

"Mom gave you that candy bar for the walk home," I said. But he didn't answer. He just kept on chomping.

"Can't he chew with his mouth closed?" Jilly asked.

"I don't think he knows how," I replied. "You should have seen him at dinner last night. We had spaghetti. He was slurping each strand into his mouth and getting gloppy spaghetti sauce all over the table."

"Gag me double!" Jilly answered.

As we got close to school, I looked back at Gregory. What he was doing now was worse than ever. He was blowing big bubbles. But the chocolate bar he'd eaten had changed the color of the gum. Instead of pink, it was all brown and lumpy. The bubbles he was blowing looked like the stuff that comes out of the kitchen sink when it's all stopped up!

"Do I dare to look over my shoulder?" Jilly asked.

"Not unless you want to barf," I warned Jilly. Gregory's cheeks puffed out and he blew a

monstrously humongous and disgusting bubble almost as big as his head. Then I heard a loud pop.

"Awk! Megan!" Gregory yelled.

"Uh-oh," Jilly said, stopping in her tracks and turning to look at him.

"Gollyoddkins!" I shouted. "What a gross mess!"

Gregory's face and hair and ears were covered with splotches of sticky, chocolatey gum. He looked like a mutant from outer space. Stringy strands of gum were dangling from his nose, ears, and eyes.

"Get it off! Get it off!" Gregory yelled as he tugged at wads of gum.

I looked at Jilly. "Don't look at me! I'm not touching that stuff," Jilly said, shaking her head. I felt the same way, but I had to help him. After all, gross or not, Gregory was my little brother. I opened my backpack and took out some tissues.

"Hurry!" Gregory yelled.

"Relax," I said as I walked over and began

to pluck pieces of chocolatey gum off of my brother. "Put your hands down, you're only making it worse."

"What's going on?" Tammy Howard and Karen Karansky asked. I was so busy working on Gregory that I didn't notice them walking over to us. Tammy and Karen are my other best friends. Tammy's the smartest girl in fifth grade and Karen is the next best athlete after me. And Jilly is the prettiest girl in our school. The four of us always hang around together. Kids at school call us the Fearsome Foursome.

"Gregory popped a bubble on his face," I explained. "And now I have to clean him up before school starts."

Tammy and Karen exchanged glances. Then they burst out laughing. I couldn't blame them. If I hadn't felt so embarrassed I might have laughed, too. A kid like Gregory was funny to everyone but his own family. I mean, a kid who burps as loud as he can in a fancy restaurant is only funny if he's not sitting at your table.

"You'd better hurry," Jilly said to me. "It's almost time for the bell. You don't want to get on the wrong side of Ms. Kramer the first day."

"I can't get this last glob of gum out of his hair," I said, trying to pry it loose.

"Ouch! That hurts!" Gregory cried as he tried to pull away from me. Just then the first bell rang.

"What am I going to do?" I sputtered.

"Let him go to class with gum in his hair," suggested Jilly.

"No! Mom would kill me," I said.

"Here," said Tammy. She pulled a small pair of scissors out of her purse. "Cut it out," she said, handing them to me.

"Let me go," Gregory grunted.

"Stand still, or I'll snip off your runny nose," I ordered. Gregory must have believed me because he stood absolutely still. I pulled the gummy clump of hair away from his head and—snip—it was gone!

"Thanks, Megan! See you after school," Gregory shouted. He picked up his lunch box

11

and backpack and dashed off toward school. He left me on the sidewalk holding a lock of gummed up hair.

"He won't be so grateful when he sees that big bare spot on the side of his head," said Karen with a laugh.

"Knowing Gregory the Gross Out, he'll probably like it and cut the other side to match," I said.

"We'd better get to class," Jilly said.

But as we started toward the building, we saw something that made us freeze in our tracks. A long, shiny black car pulled up in front of the school building. It wasn't exactly the kind of car we were used to seeing around Clover Hill School. It was a limousine, driven by a chauffeur in a uniform!

"What's a car like that doing here?" asked Jilly. We stood and stared for a second. But then the second bell rang and we had to run to our classroom. Looking over my shoulder at the limousine, the last thing I saw was the chauffeur opening the back door.

Two

WE scurried into the hall and bolted toward our classroom. We made it just before the final bell rang.

"Did you see who got out of the limo?" Tammy whispered to me.

"No," I answered. "Maybe the governor is visiting on the first day of school."

"Oh, right," she said with a laugh. "Or maybe it's the President!"

We were reviewing fractions when Ms. Thomas, the school principal, knocked on the door. She came into our room, followed by a pretty girl with long, red hair. She had on a beautiful dress that must have been expensive. It looked like the kind of dress a person who came to school in a limo would wear.

I shot a quick glance at Jilly, who sat one seat behind the empty desk across from me. Jilly's eyes widened as she raised her eyebrows. From her seat in the front of the room, Tammy turned around to look at me. And over in the row by the windows I saw Karen studying the new girl. After I studied her myself for a few seconds, I could think of only one word to describe her—perfect. Everything from her clothes to her hair was perfect. She looked like she'd just stepped out of the pages of a fashion magazine.

But it wasn't only her clothes that were perfect. If I had to stand in front of a room of strangers while two teachers were talking about me, I would have been embarrassed to death. But this new girl stood there very calmly. Wow, I thought, she's pretty cool!

"Class," said Ms. Thomas. "I would like to introduce you to a new student who's going to be in your class. This is Courtney Collins Roth. She and her family just moved to Clover Hill."

Courtney Collins Roth smiled politely. After saying a few more things to Courtney, Ms. Thomas left. Then Ms. Kramer got some text-books from the shelf and put them on the empty desk beside me. "Sit here, Courtney," Ms. Kramer said. "This is Megan Evans," she said. "And this is Jilly Duncan. The boy in front of you is Lester Babkins."

We all said hi. I felt a little sorry for the new girl because she had to sit right behind that nerdy Lester Babkins.

We finished fractions and Ms. Kramer asked us to take out our world studies book.

"That's the big, blue book," I said to Courtney as she looked through the pile of books in front of her. She smiled and nodded.

"This year we're going to study Europe and European culture," Ms. Kramer said. "Does anyone know anything about Europe?" Matthew Jenkins raised his hand.

"Europe is on the other side of the Atlantic Ocean," he said.

"That's right," said Ms. Kramer. "Has

anyone in class ever been to Europe?"

Everyone began to look around. She might as well have asked if anyone had been to Venus. Most of the kids in class, including myself, had never even been out of our state. I bet half had never even flown in an airplane. Clover Hill wasn't exactly *Lifestyles of the Rich and Famous!* But then Courtney raised her hand. "I've been to Europe, Ms. Kramer." She almost seemed a little shy about it. "I went to school in France last year."

Ms. Kramer smiled. "Courtney, would you be willing to share some of your experiences in Europe with us?" Ms. Kramer asked.

Most of us kids looked at Courtney like she had lived on another planet. Courtney sort of fidgeted in her seat. For the first time since she came in, she looked a little uncomfortable.

"I'll be glad to tell what I know about Europe," Courtney said, "...if the class really wants me to."

From the way everybody started talking,

you could tell that everyone thought it would be great to hear about Europe.

"That settles it, then," said Ms. Kramer. "From now on, part of our world studies program will include a talk by Courtney about living in Europe."

Courtney just smiled. Just like everything else about her, it was a perfect smile. I'd never met anyone like her before.

"What would you like me to talk about first?" Courtney asked the class.

"How about telling us what European kids are like," Karen called out.

"Sure. I can tell you about my roommates at boarding school. Monique was French and Ingrid was from Austria," Courtney began.

As Courtney talked, I rested my chin in my palm and listened. She was a great speaker, too. She never said "you know" or "uhh," the way most people did. As I listened to her stories about going to school in France, I decided something right then and there.

I wouldn't let anything stand in the way of

me becoming best friends with Courtney Collins Roth!

* * * * *

"That was a really good speech," I said to Courtney when we were sitting in the lunchroom.

"It sure was," added Tammy. I had introduced Courtney to Tammy and Karen. My three friends—and my new friend Courtney— were getting ready to eat lunch together.

"I really didn't mean for it to be a speech," Courtney said. "I guess I got carried away."

"Don't worry about it," said Karen. "We all loved it."

We were opening our lunch bags. I couldn't help noticing that Courtney's brown bag was tied up with a pink ribbon. She untied it quickly and stuffed the ribbon into her purse.

"Now that's what I call a fancy lunch bag!" Karen said and smiled.

"I didn't expect it to look like this," answered Courtney, looking a little embarrassed. "Our chef packed my lunch this morning."

"You mean you have a chef *and* a chauffeur?" asked Jilly.

"I guess you saw me drive up this morning in the limo," Courtney said.

"What did your chef fix you for lunch?" asked Tammy.

"Umm, let's see," Courtney answered. "Ohh," she said, looking into her bag. She sounded disappointed. "It's shrimp salad on a croissant."

She held up something that looked like a flakey hot dog bun with pink stuff dripping out of it. We just stared at it.

"Anybody want to trade?" asked Courtney.

"I just have peanut butter and jelly," I said. "You probably wouldn't like that."

"Ohh, that sounds—"

Courtney never got to finish her sentence because just then Lester Babkins came tearing down the aisle by our table. He was balancing a big plate of spaghetti on a tray.

"Hey! Watch it!" I shouted as he just missed crashing into Courtney.

"It's okay," Courtney said as Lester zoomed on by without even saying excuse me or anything.

"Some people around here have no manners," I said to Courtney. I didn't want her to think that everyone in Clover Hill was a slob. "He almost spilled that stuff all over your dress."

"I wish I hadn't worn this dress today," said Courtney. At my old school all the girls wore dresses. I wore it today because I didn't want to look different. But I goofed. I forgot how kids dress in public schools. I'll wear jeans tomorrow."

"Well, I think it would be nice if kids got more dressed up," I said. "I like your dress."

"Hey," said Tammy. "Can you imagine Lester Babkins all dressed up, coming to school in a suit?"

We all laughed and made gagging sounds— even Courtney. It felt good to see her joining in our group and laughing at the stuff we laughed at. I just knew that we'd become friends.

"What's it like to have a chauffeur and a chef?" asked Jilly.

"Well, it's okay, I guess," Courtney answered. "We have a maid and a butler, too."

Eight eyes went ga-ga all at the same time. When I snapped out of my trance, I managed to say, "I bet your mom likes having all that help around the house."

Courtney was quiet for a second. Then she said in a small voice, "Actually, my mom's not there. She's always traveling around the world and living in different hotels. I live with my dad. My parents are divorced."

"Oh, I'm sorry," I said.

Courtney just shrugged. "It's okay. They got divorced a long time ago, when I was two. My dad just moved here. He's moved around a lot. He works in real estate. On a business trip here he saw an old house he liked. So he bought it. I think it's called the Bradley estate or something like that."

"Gosh!" said Jilly. "That's the biggest house in town."

The house used to belong to old Judge Bradley. He was a politician who died last year. The house had been empty since.

"It's pretty big," was all Courtney said.

"Is that why you lived in Europe?" asked Tammy. "You lived with your mom?"

"That's right," answered Courtney. "Last year I lived with my mom and went to school in France. When my parents split up, the court decided that when I was old enough, I could live with both parents—one parent one year and the other parent the next."

I thought about what Courtney said. It would have been fun to live in Europe. But didn't she ever want to stay in one place, to make good friends? I had been friends with Jilly, Karen, and Tammy almost as long as I could remember. I couldn't stand the idea of leaving them to go live someplace else.

"I'm like a human ping-pong ball—bouncing back and forth between parents," said Courtney. "I get kind of tired of it," she said with a sad look in her eyes.

But then Courtney brightened up again and said, "This is the first time I get to go to a public school. I'm really excited about that because—"

Her words were cut off by loud screaming and yelling from a couple of tables away from us. It was coming from where the little kids sat and ate lunch.

"Look at that giant fly!" I heard a little girl yell. "Get it away from me!"

We all stood up to see what the excitement was all about. There was more screaming and shouting until things got quiet over there.

"Hey look!" said Karen.

I looked. So did the other girls. Wouldn't you know it—it was my brother Gregory crawling down the table toward where the fly had landed. He had a paper cup in his hand and was trying to catch the fly!

"Oh, no," I muttered under my breath. I

noticed that Courtney was watching him, too.

"Megan," said Jilly. "It's Gregory. He must want that fly for his dead bug collection."

"Who's Gregory?" asked Courtney.

"He's Megan's—" began Tammy.

"Neighbor!" I blurted out before Tammy could finish. "He's this kid who lives next door to me. He's really weird."

Tammy, Jilly, and Karen all gave me weird looks. But they didn't say anything about who Gregory really was.

"He got him!" shouted Courtney as Gregory whipped the paper cup over the fly, trapping it inside. The whole lunchroom clapped and cheered. All I wanted to do was dive under the table and climb through a hole in the floor.

"What's he going to do with it now?" asked Courtney. "Let it go?"

"I doubt it," I answered, trying to sink so low in my seat that no one could see me.

We all watched as Gregory took the trapped bug back to his place at the table. The fly in the cup was buzzing like mad. Then Gregory shook the cup until the fly stopped buzzing.

"I guess he knocked it out," said Jilly.

"Yuckk," said Courtney as she watched Gregory take his hand away from the top of the cup. He looked in and grinned from ear to ear. Then he reached in and plucked out the fly.

"Ughh," said Jilly.

Karen groaned.

"It must be sickening having that kid for your...neighbor," said Tammy. I gave her a dirty look.

All the first-grade girls at his table, and some of the boys, screamed as Gregory the Gross Out held up the dead fly for everybody to see.

"He's not going to eat it, is he?" asked Courtney, as Gregory lifted the fly up to his face.

"No, he probably just wants to take a closer look at it," I mumbled.

I was right. Gregory put the fly back on the table. Then he dumped his sandwich out of its plastic bag and put the fly in it to take home. He put the bag back in his lunch box. I was sure the thing would end up in that disgusting dead bug collection of his.

I closed my eyes, hoping the awful sight would go away. But when I opened them again, I saw the worst yet. Without washing the fly germs off his hands, he started eating his sandwich.

All five of us were watching him. Jilly looked a little green. Karen was holding her throat. And Tammy was making a gagging sound. Courtney didn't say anything, but the look on her face told me what she was thinking.

"Would someone show me where the girls' bathroom is?" she asked.

She was the latest victim of Gregory the Gross Out.

"Sure, I will," said Tammy.

When they had left, Jilly asked, "Why did you tell her Gregory was your neighbor?"

"Well, would you want someone like Courtney to know that you had a total gross out for a little brother?"

Jilly looked at Karen. Then she said, "Well, now that you mention it, probably not."

"Listen, you guys," I said. "I want to be friends with Courtney. If she finds out I have a creepy, slobby, gross out champion for a brother, she might not want to be around me. You have to help me keep Gregory a secret for a while."

"She'll probably find out sooner or later," said Karen.

"I know," I answered. "But later, she'll already like me and then it won't matter. We'll let her know all about him then."

"Okay, we'll help you keep him a secret," they said together.

"We'll tell Tammy about the plan," said Jilly.

"Thanks a lot, you guys," I said. "Get ready for Project Gross Out!"

Three

LATER that afternoon, I was daydreaming in class about what it would be like to have a chauffeur and a maid. Suddenly, I heard my name announced over the P.A. system.

"Megan Evans, please report to the office," Ms. Thomas announced.

I sat straight up. Did I imagine that? No, there it was again.

"Megan Evans! Please report to the office."

"I wonder what they want you for?" Jilly whispered across the aisle to me.

I shrugged my shoulders.

"Megan," said Ms. Kramer when the P.A. clicked off. "Since it's almost time to go home, you'd better take your things with you to the office."

Hurrying down the hall, I kept asking myself questions. Did I do something wrong? Am I in trouble? But as soon as I opened the door to the main office everything became clear.

"GREGORY!" I blurted out.

"Now don't be upset, Megan," said Ms. Thomas. "It looks worse than it is."

I couldn't believe my eyes. Standing with Gregory were Mrs. Clarke, the art teacher, and Ms. Riley, his regular teacher.

"He did it when we weren't looking," said Mrs. Clarke. "He was supposed to be cutting shapes out of construction paper, pasting them on a white sheet, and finger-painting around them."

"And he did *that* instead?" I gulped.

"I'm afraid so," Ms. Thomas answered.

I just stared at him. It was bad enough at lunch, with him catching that fly. But this was even worse. Gregory must have noticed that missing clump of hair that I'd cut this morning and tried to cut the other side to match. He looked like the weirdest punk-

rocker you've ever seen.

Mrs. Clarke told me what happened. During art class, Gregory had used scissors to cut off more locks of hair. The bare spots all over his head made it look like a checkerboard. On top of that, he'd used globs of paste mixed with fingerpaint to spike what was left of his hair into long, thin points of different colors.

"Gregory, how could you do this?" I asked, shaking my head.

"I look like the guy in that music video we saw last week," he answered happily. "It's cool."

"It's not cool," I told him. "It's gross! And it was a stupid thing to do."

"We phoned your mother and told her what Gregory did," Ms. Thomas said. "She asked us to have you walk him home. That's why I called you down to the office."

I nodded and took Gregory out of the office after thanking them for helping us. I was so mad that I didn't say anything at all until we were out on the playground.

"What's wrong, Megan, don't you like my

hair this way?" Gregory asked.

"No! I hate it!" I said. "And I'll die if any-body sees us." We started walking across the playground toward home.

But just then I heard a sound that made my blood run cold. It was the bell.

Doors flew open. Kids started streaming out of the school building. Soon we were surrounded by them.

"Hey! Check out that kid's head!" shouted somebody.

A crowd of older boys ran past us.

"Hey, dude!" one of them called to Gregory. "I dig your spikes!" They all laughed and laughed.

"It's goofy Gregory Evans again!" yelled a fourth grader who lived near us. Everyone who went past had something smart-alecky to say. Everybody was gaping at my brother the gross out!

Gregory thought it was great. He loved being the center of attention. And how did I feel? I was dying a slow, painful death from total embarrassment.

"Let's get out of here before anyone in fifth grade sees us," I said to my brother as I yanked on his arm. Kids were still hollering, laughing, and pointing at us as we tried to escape. When we finally got across the playground near some bushes, I felt safe.

"You're going to pull my arm off if you keep tugging on it like that," Gregory grumbled.

"Pull your arm off?" I asked. "I'd like to knock your head off, spikes and all! You always find ways to make me look like a jerk in front of my friends."

"You're the jerk, Megan," Gregory said. "If you weren't my sister I'd never even talk to you or your dippy friends."

"Good!" I snapped. "Pretend I'm not your sister. Do me a big favor. Don't talk to me for a little while...like about 10 years!"

Gregory stuck his tongue out at me.

"Let's go," I said as I started to walk. Gregory didn't answer. I stopped. "Let's go!" I said again as I turned around.

Gregory grinned at me.

"Oh, I get it," I muttered. "You're not talking to me. Well, that's fine with me. Now let's go."

Gregory didn't say a word. He just started following me. And when I turned the corner I came face to face with the one person I definitely did not want to run into. Standing there with Jilly was Courtney Collins Roth.

"Hi, Megan," said Jilly. "I told Courtney you'd probably already left. But she wanted to wait here with me until her limo gets here."

"I just wanted to say good-bye," said Courtney.

"Uhh, thanks for waiting, Courtney," I answered, smiling. She smiled back. But the smile froze on her face. It was replaced by a look of surprise or shock or horror—or disgust!

"Holy moley!" cried Courtney. "What happened to that boy's head?"

At that very moment, Gregory had come waddling around the corner looking like a punk penguin! He stopped and grinned that silly grin of his.

"Oh, no!" sputtered Jilly when she saw Gregory. "Uhh, you're walking the neighbor boy home, aren't you, Megan?" Jilly asked quickly. "We told you the kid was really, really weird, Courtney, didn't we?" Jilly nudged me with her elbow.

"Right," I nodded. "I kind of take care of him. His mom pays me to baby-sit for him and walk him home."

Courtney just stared at Gregory's red, white and blue spikes. "Whatever his mother pays you," she mumbled, "I don't think it's enough."

Gregory stood there without saying a word. It was because he told me he wouldn't talk to me or what he called my dippy friends. Well, right then, he could have called them anything he wanted, just as long as he didn't say anything to Courtney about who he really was!

"He's really not that bad of a kid," I said. "He just does a lot of goofy things."

"Yeah and he's a total gross out!" added

Jilly. Hearing that, Gregory gave her a dirty look. I thought he was going to say something. But he didn't. Instead he just smirked and started walking toward home.

"I'd better go with him," I said, glad to get away. "Thanks for waiting for me. I'll see you tomorrow."

"I have to go, too," said Jilly, as she followed me. "Bye, Courtney. See you tomorrow."

As we trotted off after Gregory, we passed Courtney's limo pulling into the parking lot. "Good-bye," Courtney called as she walked toward the limo and waved.

* * * * *

"Mom!" I yelled as I pushed Gregory through the back door of our house. "Come here and see what this crazy kid did to himself!"

Mom came into the kitchen. She looked at Gregory. Oh, boy! I thought. He's going to get it now.

37

But I couldn't believe it. Mom didn't yell at him. She burst out laughing.

"Is that a head or an American flag?" she asked.

"Mom," I said as I dropped my books. "This isn't funny."

"You don't think it's funny when your little brother comes home from school looking like the Statue of Liberty?" asked Mom.

I looked at Gregory. That little gross out had a big grin on his face.

"Mom," I said. "This has got to stop! Gregory embarrasses me every single day. I can't go on like this."

Mom sniffed. She'd laughed so hard tears were trickling down her cheeks. "I'm sorry, Megan," Mom said. "Why don't you tell me what he did to you."

"Besides that stupid hair trick," I began, "he spit all the way to school this morning."

"Spit?" asked Mom.

"Right," I said. "And at lunch, he caught a big fly in the cafeteria and packed it in his sandwich bag to bring home for his dumb dead bug collection."

"I don't do things just to make Megan mad. And besides, my bug collection is not dumb," Gregory shouted, breaking his silence.

"I thought you weren't talking to me anymore," I yelled.

"I'm not!" Gregory yelled back. "I'm talking to mom. I'm going to tell her how you lied to that red-haired girl."

I groaned.

"Lied about what?" Mom asked.

"Megan said I was the neighbors' kid," Gregory explained.

"So what?" I shot back. "I don't want my new friend to know I have a stupid brother like you."

"I'm not stupid," yelled Gregory. "You are!"

"Enough!" shouted Mom. "Gregory! Go upstairs and wash that mess out of your hair."

"But, Mom," he mumbled. "Can't I play with Morty for a while first? I want to show him my hair." Morty was Gregory's pet white mouse.

Gregory kept Morty in an old glass aquarium up in his bedroom.

"No," Mom said. "Into the shower right now. I want to get you to the barber shop before it closes so the barber can fix your hair—or what's left of it."

"Oh, all right," Gregory answered, heading upstairs.

"Now, Megan, what's all this about Gregory not being your brother?"

I took a deep breath and told Mom the whole story. I told Mom about Courtney and her dad moving into the old Bradley place, and living in France last year, and having a maid, a butler, a cook, and a chauffeur who drives a big limousine.

"It sounds like she has everything except a stable home and family," Mom said. "Is she nice?"

"She's real nice, Mom," I continued. "I want to be best friends with her. She's really cool. That's why I didn't want her to know Gregory is my brother."

"I guess they don't have little brothers in France, do they?" asked Mom. Then she gave me a serious look. "But tell me, Megan. Do you think it's right to be ashamed of your family?"

I looked down at the floor. "No, I guess it's not right," I said. "But sometimes he's just so bad. And I don't want Courtney to get the wrong impression of my family."

"Why is the truth the wrong impression?" she asked. "I mean, Gregory is your brother."

"I know." I was starting to feel a little guilty.

"How would you feel if your father and I told our friends that you weren't our daughter?" she asked.

I was getting the message, loud and clear.

"My advice to you, Miss Megan Evans," said Mom, "is that if you want Courtney to like you, then just be yourself. And being yourself means not pretending that your brother isn't related to you, no matter how weird he acts sometimes."

"You're right, Mom," I said. "I won't say that

Gregory is the neighbors' kid anymore."

I really meant what I said about not telling Courtney that Gregory the Gross Out was the neighbors' kid. But if she thought he really was the neighbors' kid, I wasn't going to tell her anything different.

Mom smiled and nodded. "That's better," she said. "And when you get to be good friends with Courtney, it won't matter that you have a little brother who sometimes does strange things. She'll like you anyway—for who you are."

As she walked upstairs to check on Gregory, I thought, *I sure hope Mom's right. But what if she's wrong?*

Four

DURING the next few weeks, Courtney and I did become better friends. In fact, the Fearsome Foursome of Tammy, Karen, Jilly, and me turned into the Fearsome Fivesome!

But we knew that Courtney was different from the rest of us, even though she tried to blend into the crowd. After that first day, Courtney rode to school on the bus and wore jeans. She even started bringing peanut butter and jelly sandwiches to lunch. But there was no way Courtney Collins Roth was an ordinary kid like the rest of us.

For example, in art class we were talking about famous painters. Courtney mentioned that her dad liked to collect paintings. After the teacher asked her some questions, it came out that the Roths have their own art gallery right in their house!

I was telling Mom and Dad all about it at dinner one night. We were having meat loaf.

"And Courtney has the nicest manners," I was saying.

"That's right," added Mom. "Megan was trying to convince me that we should use our best dishes and silverware every day."

"I know someone around here who could use some lessons in table manners," I said, looking at Gregory. He was busy burying his meat loaf under a gallon of ketchup.

"Megan," began Mom. "We've been wanting to talk to you about something. You've been talking an awful lot lately about all the things that Courtney has. I certainly hope you're not just interested in her because she's rich."

"That's right," added Dad. "Money isn't everything, you know."

I groaned. "I know it's not," I answered. "That doesn't have anything to do with it! I don't just like her because she's rich."

"It's good to hear that, dear," Mom replied. "But sometimes it sounds like you do."

What they said did make me wonder just a little bit. *Did I want Courtney to be my best friend because she was the richest kid in town?*

I didn't have much time to think about whether that was true, because I heard a disgusting slopping, slurping sound coming from the other side of the table. I looked in the direction of the sound.

It probably won't surprise you that the sound was coming from Gregory the Gross Out. He had smashed together his peas, mashed potatoes, and meat loaf. Then he had covered the whole mess with ketchup and glopped it all up together in one awful grayish, greenish, reddish goo. It looked like someone had run Mom's dinner through a blender. But that wasn't the worst part.

He had stuck his fingers in the goo and was licking them clean with his tongue. His

lips were making a horrible smacking sound.

"Make him stop that!" I screamed. Then I gagged.

"Gregory!" said Dad sternly. "Use your fork! That's not a nice thing to do at the table."

"See what I mean?" I whined. "If your friends saw that, I bet you'd tell them that Gregory was the neighbors' kid, too!"

Gregory frowned and picked up his fork. After that, he ate the right way. But I still had to look at the mess on his plate. That made it really hard to eat the rest of my dinner.

That night when Dad came up to say good-night, he told me, "You know, tomorrow is the night we go over and play cards with the Morgans."

The Morgans are our next-door neighbors. It's great when Mom and Dad go play cards there every other Friday night because they take Gregory with them to play with Bobby, their son. That leaves me alone here. I can watch TV without having to worry about you-know-who.

"Well," continued Dad, "Bobby Morgan has a Cub Scout campout, so we won't be taking Gregory with us. We thought he could just stay here with you."

"Oh, Dad," I groaned. "Jilly wanted me to spend the night."

"You'll just have to do it another time, Megan," he answered. "It's too late to find another sitter.

I gulped. It just wasn't fair. Not only did I have to watch him eat like an animal, but now I had to give up a Friday night to baby-sit for him.

"Okay," I said, "I'll do it."

"Thanks, Megan," Dad said. "We'll do something special for you to pay you back." He got up and turned out the light.

I knew they'd do something nice for me, like take me out to lunch or to the mall. My parents are great. I liked doing stuff for them, but it sure made it hard when it meant I had to give up a sleepover at Jilly's.

* * * * *

"We won't be late," Mom said on Friday night as she and Dad were getting ready to leave for the Morgans' house. "You know the number if you need us."

"Don't worry, Mom," I said as I waited at the front door. "We'll be fine—as long as Gregory listens to me."

"I'm sure he will," Dad said as he kissed me good-bye. Mom leaned over to kiss Gregory good-bye.

"Now, you be good Gregory, and do—EEK!" she shrieked.

Gregory's pet mouse, Morty, popped his head out of Gregory's shirt pocket just as Mom was about to kiss him.

"That mouse almost gave me a heart attack!" Mom gasped.

"Sorry, Mom," Gregory apologized. "I was just going to take him out for a walk."

"Well," Dad said, "make sure you put him back in his cage when he's done taking his walk. And be sure to behave for Megan while we're gone."

"Okay, Dad," Gregory said. He took Morty back upstairs.

Mom kissed me good-bye. "Thanks again for baby-sitting," she said.

Dad smiled and winked at me as he opened the front door. "Remember, I owe you a favor."

I stood in the doorway and watched them go down the walk. Then I shut the door and locked it. Just as I headed for the living room to turn on the TV, the telephone rang. I walked over to the phone on the table in the hall and picked up the receiver. It was Jilly.

"Hi!" I said, leaning back against the wall and sliding down to the floor.

"How about that bracelet Courtney wore to school today?" Jilly asked. "I bet those were real diamonds!"

"She said it was a birthday present from her mom last year. It must have cost a fortune," I said.

"Megan, where are you? I'm hungry,"

Gregory yelled from the kitchen.

"Quiet," I said. "I'm on the phone. I'll get you something to eat when I'm finished talking to Jilly."

"By the time you finish talking to that dippy Jilly, I'll starve to death," Gregory said.

"Hold on a second, Jilly," I said. "You-know-who is bugging me." I put the phone down. "You'll have to wait," I said to Gregory. "The reason you're so hungry is because you didn't eat your dinner."

"The reason I didn't eat it is because it was disgusting," Gregory said.

"Of course it was disgusting," I fired back. "Only an idiot would put mustard on tuna casserole!"

"I'm hungry," Gregory kept hollering.

"Well, if you can't wait until I'm finished talking, go into the kitchen and make yourself a snack," I shouted.

Gregory walked into the kitchen.

"Okay, Jilly," I said into the phone. "Now, where were we?"

"We were talking about Courtney's brace-let," she said.

"Oh, yeah," I said. "I bet everything in her house cost plenty."

"Hey, I've got an idea," Jilly said. "Why don't you, Karen, Tammy, and I ride by the Bradley house on our bikes tomorrow."

"Great idea!" I agreed.

"I'll tell Karen and Tammy about it when they get here tonight," Jilly said.

"Okay," I said. "I'll come over to your house at noon. We'll leave from there."

Right then I heard a loud crash and a howl from the kitchen. "Uh-oh! I've got to go!" I said. "See you tomorrow, Jilly."

I hung up the phone and scrambled to my feet. I dashed into the kitchen.

"GOLLYODDKINS!" I cried when I saw what had happened.

The kitchen looked like a food bomb had exploded! But it was no bomb—only my brother the gross out.

The room was a complete disaster area. The

refrigerator door was wide open. A container of grape juice was dripping down the shelves and splattering into a big, purple puddle. Near the spill on the floor was a carton of eggs. The broken eggs looked like big, yellow eyes staring up at me.

And that was just the floor.

The kitchen table was the biggest mess of all. A loaf of bread was ripped open and slices of white bread were scattered around like playing cards. Lots of jars were cluttered in the middle of the table. Each jar had a spoon or a fork stuck in it.

Standing on a kitchen chair holding a sloppy sandwich oozing with ketchup was Gregory.

"I made myself a peanut butter, pickle, and ketchup sandwich," Gregory announced. He pointed at the floor. "Some stuff fell out of the refrigerator."

"Gregory!" I yelled. "Look at this mess! Who's going to clean it up?"

Gregory bit into his gross sandwich and

shrugged his shoulders. Yucky gunk was oozing out of the sides of the bread. "I told you I was hungry," he answered, chewing with his mouth open.

"I'll tell you who's going to clean this up!" I said. "You are—or I'll tell Mom!"

"You told me to fix my own snack. So I did," Gregory said.

Hmm, he was right about that. I guess it was partly my fault after all.

"Okay," I said with a sigh, "I'll clean it up." I went to get a bucket and some sponges from the cabinet under the sink.

Gregory put his sloppy sandwich on the table. "I'll help," he said. "We'll clean it up together, Megan."

I had to smile. "For somebody who's so gross, maybe you're not so bad after all," I said.

Gregory took out a roll of paper towels and started wiping off the refrigerator.

"Just think," I said. "If we had a maid like Courtney Collins Roth does, we'd never have to do stuff like this!"

Five

O N Saturday morning, Jilly, Karen, and Tammy were waiting on their bikes outside of Jilly's house when I pedaled up. "Hi," I said as I coasted to a stop. "Are you guys ready to go?"

"We sure are," Jilly said. We pushed off and started riding down the road.

As we rode through town, we talked about what Courtney's house might be like.

"I'll bet it's as nice as any of the houses on that show about the rich and famous," said Karen.

"Or even better!" added Jilly. We passed Lester Babkins' house. Lester was mowing his front lawn. He made a face at us as we rode by. We pretended not to see him.

"It's only a few more blocks to the Bradley estate," Tammy said.

We rode for a few more minutes. Then Tammy cried out, "There it is!"

The old Bradley estate was in the fanciest part of Clover Hill. It was at the very end of Paradise Lane, a dead-end road that had only two other houses on it. The mayor lived in one and the president of the local bank lived in the other.

The place was a gigantic, three-story brick house. It had a greenhouse behind the main house and gardens all around the grounds. There was a fish pond, a putting green, a swimming pool, and who knows what else.

"Gollyoddkins," I said. "There's enough room in that house for all of our families to live!"

"And it's just Courtney and her dad living there," said Karen.

"Don't forget all the servants," added Jilly.

We stopped our bikes at the private drive that led up to the house. There was no one around except a man in dusty old clothes working in the flower beds along the driveway.

"What a mansion!" sighed Karen.

"There's only one word for this place," said Jilly. "Unbelievable!"

For a few minutes, we all just stood there, silently staring at the home of Courtney Collins Roth.

"Hi, girls. Can I help you?" We turned to see the guy who had been working in the flower beds standing beside us.

"Uhh...we were just looking," I sputtered.

"Oh," replied the man. He had smudges of dirt on his face. "Go right ahead, look all you want."

"What's the owner like?" Jilly blurted out. "Is he a good guy to work for?"

The man laughed. "He's a decent guy, I guess," he answered.

"Is it a hard job to be a gardener?" Tammy asked. "Does the butler boss you around or anything?"

The man laughed again. "No," he said. "The butler doesn't give me too many orders. I don't have to take out the garbage or anything."

"It's not that we're prying or anything," I said to the man. "We go to school with the owner's daughter, Courtney. Do you know her?"

"Yes, I do know her," the gardener said.

"We were...well...we were..."

"You were wondering what kind of person her father is," the man finished for me.

"Well...yes," I admitted.

"I think you'd like him," the man replied with a smile. "Shall I go tell Miss Roth that you're here to visit?"

"NO!" Jilly said quickly.

"NO!" we all echoed.

"We have to go," Tammy said.

"Thanks for talking to us," I said to the gardener as we got back on our bikes. "And please, please, whatever you do, don't tell Courtney—I mean Miss Roth—that we were here asking questions."

"All right, I promise I won't," chuckled the man. We waved and rode back toward town.

"He was nice," Tammy said as we pedaled down Paradise Lane. "And Courtney's father sounds nice, too."

"Let's go back to my house for cookies and lemonade," I said.

Everyone thought that was a great idea. We reached my house in record time. We parked our bikes on the front lawn and went around the back of the house to the patio. "Have a seat," I said to the girls. "I'll get the cookies and lemonade." Suddenly, we heard a rustling sound in the bushes next to the patio.

"What's that?" asked Jilly as she pointed at the shaking bushes.

"There's something in there," I said.

"Maybe it's a raccoon," muttered Tammy.

"Maybe it's a skunk," mumbled Karen.

All of a sudden a white mouse with pink eyes came scrambling out of the shrubs and bolted across the patio.

"It's Gregory's mouse!" I yelled. Morty sat up on his hind legs, wiggled his nose, and squeaked at all of us.

We heard some more rustling in the bushes. "I have a feeling we're going to get a look at another wild animal," I said.

Sure enough, my brother poked his grinning head out of the bushes.

"Get that mouse out of here!" I ordered.

"Okay, okay. He's just getting some fresh air," said Gregory as he climbed out of the bushes. He walked over to Morty and picked him up.

I opened the sliding doors for Gregory and he took Morty into the house. "I'll be right back with our snacks," I said as I went in after Gregory.

Before I shut the door, I heard Karen say, "That Gregory is the grossest kid I know. Having a brother like him must be a constant pain in the neck!"

When I came back with the cookies and lemonade on a tray, who do you think was sitting in my chair? Three guesses.

"Help yourselves," I said to my friends as I put the pitcher on the patio table.

"What about me?" yelled Gregory.

"You can have some," I said. "Just calm down."

"Oh, boy! Chocolate-chip cookies," said Karen as she took a cookie. Jilly and Tammy also took one cookie each.

"Don't I get any?" asked Gregory.

I offered him the tray. Instead of taking one, he grabbed a whole fistful.

"Where are your manners?" I asked, pulling the tray back from him. I put the cookies on the table and took one for myself. In the time it took us to finish our one cookie each, Gregory had gobbled up all four of his.

"Seconds anyone?" I asked. "Or fifths, if anybody here has already had four?" I gave Gregory a dirty look.

Before Tammy, Karen, and Jilly could take another cookie, Gregory scooted over to the cookie tray. Just as he was about to grab

another handful of cookies, he stopped. His face twisted up and his nose started to twitch.

"No, you little creep," I shouted. "No!"

I made a grab for him to pull him away from the cookies. But I was too late.

"Ah-ah-ah-CHOO!"

Gregory the Gross Out sneezed all over the cookie tray! That awful sneeze will definitely go into his Grossness Hall of Fame!

Karen looked sick. "On second thought I think I've had enough cookies," she muttered.

"Me too," mumbled Tammy.

"Me three," sighed Jilly. "But that first cookie sure was good."

I just stood there, boiling mad. I was actually too mad to even talk.

"If no one wants to eat the rest of these, I guess I'll eat them," said Gregory. He scooped up the rest of the cookies and waddled into the house.

*　*　*　*　*

We were all eating lunch together at school the next Monday.

"Does anybody want some chocolate-chip cookies?" I asked, unwrapping my bag and pushing them to the middle of the table.

"Thanks," said Courtney. She took a cookie and began to nibble on it. "They're great."

I noticed that no one else took one. Then I remembered what happened on Saturday.

"Don't worry, you guys," I said. "These are sneeze-proof."

Karen, Jilly, and Tammy laughed, and each took a cookie.

"Sneeze-proof?" asked Courtney. "What does that mean?"

"Oh, umm, it's just an old joke," I explained. "It's really nothing important."

"Oh," Courtney answered. She tried to smile, but I could tell she felt left out because she didn't understand the joke. I decided to try not to say anything else that would make her feel left out.

Luckily, Tammy changed the subject just then and we talked about school and cute boys and other stuff.

Then Karen asked me if I was going to try out for the basketball team again this year. Last year, I was sort of the star of the team.

I looked at Courtney and then said, "Oh, I might. I haven't decided yet."

"What?!?" asked Jilly. "What do you mean you haven't decided yet? You're the biggest basketball nut in Clover Hill. You just told me last week you'd do anything to get Michael Jordan's autograph!"

I gave Jilly a dirty look.

"Well," I said. "Basketball's okay. But I don't think it's as cool as...uhh...tennis or golf or...or...polo." I tried to think of all the sports that rich people play.

"Do you play tennis?" Courtney asked me.

"Uhh, yeah, a little bit," I answered. Actually, I had hit an old ball against the garage a couple of times. "I'm learning."

"What's with tennis?" Tammy asked me. "You're the best girls' basketball player at Clover Hill School."

Courtney looked at me in a strange way.

"I only play so I'll get an *A* in gym," I blurted out. "Uhh, Courtney. Isn't it your turn to go get the milk?" We all took turns getting the milk. I reached into my pocket and handed Courtney my milk money.

"Yes, I guess it is my turn," she said. She collected money from the other girls and walked up to the milk line.

When Courtney was gone, Tammy, Jilly, and Karen all looked at me. "What's going on about not liking basketball?" Karen asked.

I shrugged. "Courtney will think I'm just an ordinary kid if she finds out I like basketball," I explained.

"But Megan, you *are* an ordinary kid," Jilly reminded me. "We all are."

"I know," I answered. "But Courtney isn't an ordinary kid. She's used to the finer things in life. Do you think she's going to want to be friends with a bunch of nerds who like to dribble basketballs around a smelly gym?"

The girls glanced at each other. "But that's what we like to do," said Tammy.

"Yeah, she's going to find out sooner or later what we're like," added Jilly.

"And why are you trying to hide who you really are?" asked Karen. "You never used to be ashamed."

"Besides," added Jilly, "we like you the way you are. You don't have to make up stories about yourself."

"I know that," I said. "But I just think if she finds out later it will be better for us. Let's break it to her gently about how normal we are. After she likes us, then it won't matter that we like basketball and stuff like that."

They were all shaking their heads.

"Well, I don't like it one bit," said Tammy.

"Neither do I," added Karen. "I'm not ashamed of the way I am. I'm not rich. I can't help it. Maybe you don't want to be friends with me anymore—I'm *soooo* ordinary!"

"You know that's not true!" I shouted. The kids at the next table looked over at me. I lowered my voice. "I'm not ashamed of us. I just want her to think that we're the kind of kids she would want to be friends with, that's all."

"I like Courtney, too," said Jilly. "But I think it would be better if we just tried to be ourselves."

"Shh, here she comes," whispered Tammy.

"Milk delivery," announced Courtney as she put the milk on the table. She sat down and asked, "What did you guys do this weekend?"

"Well, on Saturday," Karen said, "we went bike riding."

"Oh," said Courtney, "that sounds like fun."

"It was," Jilly answered. "If you want, we can call you next time we go."

"I'd like that a lot," Courtney said.

"What did you do, Courtney?" asked Tammy.

"Oh, not much," Courtney answered. I started reading a new book. It's about these twin sisters who have a terrible little brother."

That made me think about my own

brother, Gregory the Gross Out. Maybe if I had a twin sister, I could handle him better!

"Then I watched some TV," continued Courtney. "The book was good, but my weekend was basically boring. I haven't had any real fun in a while.

Then Courtney smiled. "Hey! I've got an idea," she said. "Why don't the four of you come over to my house next Friday for a sleepover?"

"Boy, that's a great idea!" I said right away. "I'd love to. I'm sure my parents will let me come."

Jilly, Tammy, and Karen nodded.

"Okay, then it's all settled," announced Courtney.

Six

THE week dragged by. I couldn't think of anything else except the sleepover on Friday at the mansion of Miss Courtney Collins Roth.

When we were finally in the car, driving to Courtney's house, I was almost floating. I kept pinching myself to make sure I wasn't dreaming. Would I be waited on by a butler and a maid? Would I get to sleep in satin sheets and get breakfast in bed? It was all just too totally awesome!

As usual, my fantasy was shattered by the sight of Gregory the Gross Out. He was sitting beside me in the backseat. I hadn't been paying any attention to him, and he had been very quiet. When I looked at him, I knew why.

He'd been eating a chocolate bar. And from the looks of him, I'd say he might even have gotten some of it in his mouth. Most of the chocolate bar was all over his face and hands.

"Mom!" I yelled as I slid to the other side of the car to get as far away from Gregory as I could. "Look at him. He's a mess!"

Mom turned around to look at Gregory. He smiled and held up his chocolately hands.

"Gregory! How many times have I told you— no candy before dinner!"

Then that little gross out started to reach for me with his chocolatey hands. He wiggled his messy fingers.

"Touch me and you die!" I screamed.

"Keep your hands to yourself, young man," Dad ordered. Gregory lowered his hands.

Mom gave Gregory some tissues and he began to clean himself up.

"What if he gets chocolate on my dress?" I whined.

"He won't," said Mom calmly. How she can stay so calm with Gregory for a kid I'll never understand. "You won't, will you, Gregory?"

Gregory acted like he was thinking about it. Then he finally said, "No, I don't think so."

"He's going to drive me insane one of these days!" I said. I scooted over even closer to the window and looked out, trying to forget the little terror just a few inches away from me.

"Well, here we are," Dad finally announced as he pulled into the driveway leading to the Roths' house.

"This is a beautiful house!" Mom said.

When Dad stopped the car I pulled out my overnight bag. "Bye, Dad. You don't have to pick me up. I'll walk home on Saturday."

"Have a good time," he said.

Gregory was making a gross face at me through the window. I ignored him. Mom and I got out and walked up to the front door.

"The butler will probably answer the door," I said to Mom.

But when the door opened I was surprised. The man who answered the door wasn't dressed in a butler's suit. He was wearing normal clothes. What was even weirder was that he was the same guy we saw working in the garden the week before.

"Hi," the man said with a smile. "Come on in. You must be Megan. And you must be her mother. I'm Reginald T. Roth."

I almost died on the spot, thinking about what we said to Courtney's dad when we thought he was a servant! I know my face must have turned as red as an apple.

Mr. Roth took my overnight bag and led us into the hallway. To me, it looked about as big as a football field.

"Thank you, Mr. Roth," Mom said as we walked in. I just stared in awe. My jaw almost dropped to the floor. It was like stepping into a fairy tale. There was even a real suit of armor standing in the hall.

"Call me Rusty," Mr. Roth said to my mom.

"Okay, Rusty," Mom answered. "My name is Judy. Welcome to Clover Hill."

"Thank you, Judy," Mr. Roth said. "Clover Hill is a very nice town. My daughter loves it here." Just then Courtney came into the hallway. I was surprised to see that she was dressed in jeans and a blouse.

"Hi, Megan," said Courtney. "You look great. That's a pretty dress. Is this your mom?"

I introduced Mom and Courtney. After a little more talking, Mom said good-bye and left.

"You're welcome here anytime," Mr. Roth said to me with a wink. Then I knew he'd kept his promise and hadn't told Courtney about our visit last weekend.

"Come on," he said. "Let's not leave the other guests alone too long." He picked up my overnight bag and led us into a nearby sitting room. On the way I had a chance to look at some of the house. It was definitely good enough to be on that show about the rich and famous. I could just imagine that guy with the weird voice wandering through the house and pointing out neat stuff.

"Look who's here, ladies," said Mr. Roth as we went into the sitting room. Jilly, Karen, and Tammy smiled up at me.

"Now the party can officially start," Courtney said. "Everyone's here."

I saw that Jilly, Karen, and Tammy were all wearing their best dresses, too. We had all made the same mistake, thinking that Courtney would wear a fancy dress. At least we had all goofed!

"I hate to run out on five beautiful girls," said Mr. Roth, "but I have to go on a business trip."

"Do you really have to go, Dad?" asked Courtney. She sounded disappointed.

"Yes, hon, you know I do," said Mr. Roth as he kissed Courtney on the forehead. "I have to go look at a building in San Francisco. I'll be back in two days. Rollins will keep an eye on you. If you need anything, just ask him.

Mr. Roth turned to us. "Bye, girls," he said, waving. "Have a good time." Then he left the room.

I went up to Courtney. "He'll only be gone for two days," I said. She shrugged her shoulders and forced herself to smile.

"It's always two days here, three days there," she said. "Sometimes I wish I had a brother or sister to keep me company."

"We'll keep you company," said Jilly.

Courtney looked at us. "I'm sorry to complain about it to you guys. I guess I should be used to it by now," she said.

"Don't be sorry. That's what friends are for," Tammy said.

Courtney smiled. And this time it seemed like a real smile. "What do you want to do first?" she asked.

"How about a tour of the house?" asked Jilly.

"I'd love to see your art gallery," I said.

"Okay," said Courtney. "Follow me! I hope I can find my way around. I'm still not used to this house."

We started upstairs. Courtney led us through one beautiful bedroom after another. The house had six giant bedrooms and each one was furnished in a different way. One was modern. Another was colonial. Another was Oriental. It looked like a fabulous museum.

"I love that each bedroom has its own bathroom," said Tammy. "We only have one bathroom and my big brothers are always hogging it!"

The last room we saw was Courtney's. Her bedroom was the best room of all, even though it was a little messy. It had a huge, white canopy bed in the center of the room and lots of other nice furniture that all matched. On the wall were posters of rock stars, movie stars, and TV personalities. There was even a poster of Larry Bird, the pro basketball player.

"I'm sorry about my room," Courtney said. "It's a total disaster."

I wondered why the maid didn't come in and clean it up. Maybe the maid was on vacation or something. They got vacations, didn't they?

We went back downstairs and Courtney showed us the formal dining room first. It was humongous. The table looked big enough to land an airplane on. Next we visited her dad's den. There were a ton of books on shelves all around the room, and paintings, photos, and statues all over the place.

After the den we walked through the sitting room, the living room, the front parlor, and the kitchen. We met Mr. Todd, the chef, who was busy preparing dinner.

"What are we having for dinner?" Karen whispered to Courtney. "Pheasant? Caviar?"

Courtney laughed. "No, I hate that stuff! We're having burgers and fries. I hope that's okay. That's what my dad and I always have on Friday nights."

"That sounds great," Karen answered.

"Sure, that's fine," I repeated. But I was a little surprised. I'd kind of expected us to have a big, fancy sit-down dinner.

"The next stop on the tour," announced Courtney, "is the art gallery."

We followed Courtney down a corridor off the kitchen.

"Here it is," she said, opening some doors.

The art gallery was even better than I'd expected. It had to be the biggest room in the house. There were more paintings than I could count on the walls. There were drawings and sculptures, too. We oohed and aahed our way around the room. The funniest part of the tour was when Tammy pointed to a statue of some Greek god who was wearing only a leaf.

"I guess he doesn't have much of a laundry bill," said Jilly as we walked by.

After we left the art gallery, we went into a room Courtney said was her favorite place in the house. It was the Roths' entertainment center. It was kind of like a millionaire's play-room. The first thing we noticed was a huge, wide-screen TV in the corner.

"Wow!" Jilly said when she saw it. "This is like going to a drive-in movie—without a car!"

In another corner were some video games and a pinball machine.

"It's just like an arcade," Karen said, "except everything is free."

There was also a juke box, a ping-pong

table, and a pool table.

"You don't have a bowling alley hidden in the closet, do you?" I asked Courtney.

She laughed and shook her head. "No, but if you suggest it to my dad, he might put one in the basement!" she joked.

Just then the butler appeared in the doorway. Courtney introduced him to us. His name was Rollins and he was dressed exactly like I expected a butler to be dressed.

"Dinner is ready, Miss Courtney," Rollins announced. "Shall I serve it in here?"

Courtney looked at us. "Is that okay with you guys?" she asked.

"Super," called Karen, without looking up from the video game she was playing.

The rest of us agreed and before we knew it, Rollins had served us dinner. We sat at a small table and ate everything.

"After dinner would you please take my friends' bags up to their rooms, Rollins?" Courtney asked the butler.

"Of course, Miss," he answered.

After the meal we spent the rest of the night doing typical sleepover stuff. I say typical, but the way we did the stuff wasn't really typical.

We watched movies on the huge TV—the movies were from the Roths' film library. Courtney said they had 700 movies! Rollins served us popcorn and drinks whenever we wanted, so we didn't even have to get up.

Around 9:00, Rollins brought us a pizza made by Chef Todd. It was the best pizza I'd ever had. After Rollins went to bed, we changed into pajamas and sat around blabbing. We talked about everything and everyone, from the leaky faucet in the girls' restroom at school to Lester Babkins.

When it was finally time to go to bed, we each went to our own rooms. That was the first time I had ever done that at a sleepover. As I lay in that huge bed in my own luxurious room, one thing kept running through my mind. I even said it out loud.

"I think I could get to like being rich. This is definitely the life!"

Seven

THE next morning a light knock at my door woke me up. I had been having a beautiful dream about how my mom and dad had just won the state lottery and collected $12 million!

"Breakfast in 20 minutes, Miss Evans," said Rollins.

"Thank you," I answered as I hopped out of bed. I washed up in my private bathroom and got dressed. I had brought a couple of different outfits with me. I decided to wear a pair of dress jeans and a nice top. I wanted to look nice but not overdressed.

Before I left the room I looked at the unmade bed. Hmm, I wondered, should I make it? Or should I just leave it? I started toward the bed and then stopped. I decided the maid was probably supposed to make the beds. I left it as it was.

I opened the door to my room and went out into the hall. I bumped right into Jilly, whose room was across the hall from mine.

"Good morning, Miss Duncan," I said, trying to sound like the butler. "Did you sleep well?"

"Yes," she answered. "Thank you, Rollins. I slept like a princess."

We giggled quietly. Then I said, "Hey, Jilly. Did you make your bed?"

"No," she answered. "Did you?"

I shook my head. "Are we supposed to?"

Jilly shrugged her shoulders.

Just then Karen came out into the hall. "What's all the whispering about?" she asked.

We were about to tell her when Courtney came up the stairs. "Hi, you guys," she said.

Then Tammy came out of her room and the five of us went downstairs for breakfast. It was served buffet-style in the dining room, just like a fancy restaurant.

"Look at all this food," Jilly whispered to me.

We all helped ourselves and sat down at the big table. We talked about the house and how nice our bedrooms were. Suddenly Tammy let out a little squeal. Out of the corner of my eye, I saw a sausage go flying off the table and land on the floor with a loud plop!

Poor Tammy turned red, she was so embarrassed. You would have thought she dropped a bomb instead of a sausage. We all sat there in silence as the sausage rolled and rolled.

But then Courtney burst out laughing. We all started laughing after that, even Tammy.

"I'll get it," Courtney said as she hopped off her chair. She picked up the runaway sausage and put it on the table.

After we all stopped giggling, Karen said, "You wouldn't have to do that at my house. Our dog, Spike, eats everything that falls on the floor."

That made us all start laughing again. "I wish I could have a pet," Courtney said. "But I can't because I move around so much." She looked at Karen. "What kind of dog is Spike?"

"He's just a mutt," Karen said.

"I've heard they're the best kind," Courtney answered.

"You wouldn't say that if you saw Spike," said Jilly. "That hound could take first place in an ugly dog contest!"

"You have a sister *and* a pet, Karen," Courtney said. "I bet you're never lonely."

"I never get five minutes to be alone, so how can I be lonely?" Karen asked. "If Spike isn't following me around looking for food, my little sister, Marsha, is bugging me."

I wondered how Courtney would feel about being lonely if she were stuck with Gregory the Gross Out? One look at his dead bug collection or his awful ketchup sandwiches would have changed her mind. I decided I'd trade her Gregory for Rollins the butler any day.

"If everyone's finished eating, we can take a walk around the grounds," said Courtney. "The gardens and trees are really pretty at this time of the year."

We all followed her outside. Courtney was right. The gardens were beautiful. We took a long walk. We looked at the goldfish in the pond. And after that we spent some more time in the entertainment center playing games and watching TV.

The morning zoomed by and before we knew it, it was time to go home—back to normal life. The four of us said thanks about a million times. We turned to wave at the end of the long driveway.

"That sure was a great time," said Tammy. We all agreed with her as we walked down the street.

"I wish we could pay Courtney back somehow," said Jilly.

Karen nodded. "Maybe we could have a party for her at one of our houses," she suggested.

"Good idea," Jilly agreed.

"Hey! Why don't we have a welcome to Clover Hill party for Courtney next Friday night?" Tammy asked as we turned right at the

end of Paradise Lane.

I stopped. "That's a good idea," I said. "But whose house are we going to use?"

"My house is too much of a zoo with Spike barking all the time and Marsha poking her nose into everything," Karen said. "We wouldn't have any privacy."

"My mom's going to be gone on a business trip," Tammy said. "And we're having a baby-sitter."

"Yuck," we all said. Scratch Tammy's house.

"My house would be perfect," Jilly explained, "except my brother and sister are coming home from college next week and the place will be too crowded."

All eyes looked at me. That left only one place where we could have the party.

"Forget Megan's house," said Tammy. "Do I have to remind you of a little problem called Gregory the Gross Out?"

"Yeah, don't forget Gregory," I said. "It looks like we'll just have to do it some other time."

"Wait a minute," Jilly cried. "Megan, don't

your parents play cards at the neighbors'
house every other Friday night?"

"That's right," I said. Then I understood
what she was getting at.

"Gollyoddkins!" I exclaimed. "Next Friday is
their night to play again."

"So?" asked Tammy. "What's that got to do
with Gregory?"

"Gregory always goes with my folks," I
explained. "We'd have the house to ourselves!
Mom and Dad would let us stay by ourselves
because they'll just be next door."

The rest of the walk home, we talked about
the party. It would be perfect. We'd all help to
fix food and clean up the house and make
decorations. We'd all chip in to buy Courtney
a welcome present. And Tammy would make
her Aunt Aggie's fancy little sandwiches. It
would be fantastic.

"All right," I said as we split up at the corner
to go to our houses. "It's all set. This'll be the
greatest party in the history of Clover Hill!"

Eight

I almost jumped for joy when my parents agreed to let me have the party for Courtney. At first Dad didn't like the idea of me having a party while he and mom were out of the house. But Mom convinced him that everything would be all right, especially since they were going to be right next door.

On Saturday night I phoned Tammy, Karen, and Jilly to tell them the good news.

"Karen and Tammy said they'd come over every day after school next week to help me clean," I told Jilly. As usual, I was sitting on the floor in the hall while I talked on the phone.

All of a sudden Gregory came crawling out of the living room on his hands and knees. With his eyes glued to the floor, he thumped

past me. It was so weird, even for him, that I was a little curious.

"Hold on a second, Jilly," I said. I covered the phone with my hand. "Gregory, what are you doing?" I asked.

Gregory stopped crawling. He glanced up at me. "I'm looking for something," he told me.

"What?" I asked.

"A spider," he answered, "a big, black, hairy one. It just crawled out here from under the couch. I want it for my dead bug collection."

"Yeow!" I screeched, hopping to my feet. I dropped the phone.

"What's wrong?" yelled Mom as she ran out into the hall.

"Megan is afraid of a spider," Gregory explained. He kept looking for it. "She's not a sister. She's a sissy!"

"Gregory, get off the floor this instant," Mom ordered. "I'll get the bug spray."

"Ohh," groaned Gregory as he stormed off down the hall. "Now you've ruined everything,

Megan. I'll get you for this."

Keeping an eye out for the spider, I picked the phone up off the floor. "Jilly?" I asked. "Are you still there?"

"Yes," she answered. "What happened? I heard a scream."

"Gregory the Gross Out was at it again, that's all," I answered as Mom returned, clutching a can of bug spray. "Jilly, I'll talk to you tomorrow after I call Courtney tonight and invite her to the party."

I hung up the phone and scooted out of the hallway. I didn't want to be anywhere near there if that big, hairy spider turned up!

When I called Courtney that night to tell her about the party, I thought she seemed a little—well—unexcited about the party. It wasn't like she didn't want to come. But I was a little disappointed that she didn't seem too psyched up for it.

For a second I thought maybe she was afraid that our party wouldn't be fancy enough for her. After all, Jilly was right. We *are* just ordinary kids. Maybe Courtney only liked parties at the mansions of other rich kids. I decided that we'd have to make our party as nice and fancy as we could. Then we'd be sure that Courtney thought we were the kind of kids she was used to hanging around with!

When I was walking to my room to start making a list of everything we'd need for the party, I glanced into Gregory's room. What a big mistake!

Gregory was sitting on his bed, surrounded by a bunch of shoe boxes. I knew what was in those boxes—his awful dead bug collection. He had each bug stuck to a cardboard sheet with a long pin.

After a few seconds Gregory noticed me standing in the doorway. I couldn't believe what that horrible little creature did next.

"Hey, Megan," he said. "I know what you can have to eat at your party."

"Yeah? What?"

He held up a big, hairy spider on a pin. It must have been the one that Mom had killed in the hallway with her bug spray. On the pin, it looked a little bit like a party appetizer.

Then Gregory pretended to eat the spider on the long pin. He smacked his lips after he pretended to eat it and said, "Mmm, mmm, very tasty."

I gagged and stomped into my room. I slammed the door as hard as I could.

On Tuesday, Jilly and I went shopping for Courtney's present. We found a little china statue of a ballerina. The saleslady put it in a pretty, pink box and wrapped it up. It was just about the prettiest package I'd ever seen.

"It's perfect. She's going to love it," Jilly said as we walked home.

The next day all of my friends came over to start housecleaning. Did we ever clean!

We dusted! We mopped! We polished! We vacuumed everything in sight! Then we dusted, mopped, polished, and vacuumed everything again!

"You're ruining the house," Gregory complained as we were working upstairs one day.

He stood watching us work, twirling a squirt gun on his finger.

"There won't be a spider web left in the house. And no spider webs means no bugs for my bug collection," Gregory whined.

"You've got too many bugs already," Jilly said.

"You're right," he said. "I even need more boxes. My bugs are too crowded."

"What a kook," Jilly said after Gregory had walked off, probably to look for more bugs. "It's a good thing he's going to be out of the house on Friday night."

"You're not kidding," I answered.

Nine

WHEN Friday night finally came and the house was all ready for the party, Jilly, Tammy, Karen, and I stood gazing at the table of food. Mom and Dad and Gregory were upstairs getting ready to go over to the Morgans' to play cards.

"Gollyoddkins!" I said. "I can't believe how great everything looks!"

The punch bowl was filled with ice, fruit, and a special grape punch my dad helped us make. Around it were trays filled with all sorts of tasty treats—little sandwiches, chips and dip, cookies, cheese cubes, and lots of other things.

"All that delicious food is making my mouth water," said Karen. "I have to eat something."

She reached out to take a cracker topped with cheese spread and an olive.

"Oh, no, you don't!" I ordered, moving in front of Karen. "This table is perfect. And it has to stay perfect until Courtney sees it. If you take away even one cracker, it won't look as good. You'll just have to wait until the party starts."

"Okay, okay," Karen said. "But I'm starving. Give me something to do to take my mind off the food."

"Umm, why don't you go up to my room and get Courtney's present?" I suggested.

"Right," said Karen as she headed upstairs.

The rest of us puttered around putting finishing touches on everything. Tammy put the tray of fancy little sandwiches in the fridge to keep them cool. We must have been pretty nervous because we couldn't sit still for a minute.

"I didn't get anything on my white dress, did I?" I asked Tammy and Jilly for about the tenth time.

"No!" answered Jilly. "You look perfect. The food is perfect. The house is perfect. You're acting like it's the President of the United States coming over, not just another girl in our class."

"Jilly!" I said in a loud voice. "She's not just another girl in our class! You've been to her house yourself, so you should know that!"

Jilly looked angry. "I'm not sure this party is such a good idea," she said. "Maybe I don't want to stay."

I felt really bad all of a sudden. "Jilly," I said, plopping down on the couch. "I'm sorry. I guess I'm a little nervous about everything being perfect. I didn't mean to yell at you." But she just turned around and walked into the kitchen to help Tammy with some glasses.

What was wrong with me? Here I was yelling at my best friend for no reason. This whole thing was really getting on my nerves. It sure was tough trying to be perfect so you could make friends with the new rich girl!

I didn't have any more time to feel sorry for

myself because Karen was just coming down-stairs with the present.

"We're lucky I went upstairs when I did," Karen said. "Gregory was fooling around with the present."

"What?" I shrieked. "Is it okay?"

"Yes, it's fine," Karen said. Tammy and Jilly came into the dining room when they heard me scream.

"I found him coming out of his room with it," Karen continued. "I practically had to pull it away from him."

"He didn't open it, did he?" Jilly sputtered.

"Don't worry," Karen said. "The ribbon's just a little crooked and wrinkled, that's all. I fixed it."

"Phew!" I sighed. "That was close. He can mess things up faster than anyone I know."

"Speaking of Gregory," said Tammy, "are you ever going to tell Courtney you have a brother?"

"Shh," I said softly, looking upstairs. I could hear Mom and Dad coming down. "Don't mention that, or I'll get in trouble with my parents. Don't worry, I'll tell Courtney about Gregory—sooner or later."

"We're about ready to go," said Dad as he walked into the dining room with my little brother. "Your mother is calling the Morgans right now to say we're on our way." Gregory was carrying his squirt gun. He pretended to aim it at the food table.

"Stop it, Gregory," Dad said calmly. "Boy, everything looks fantastic," he added.

"Look at all the food!" Gregory said, starting toward the table.

"Forget it!" I yelled. I rushed over to block his way.

"But I'm hungry," groaned Gregory.

"I don't care. Eat at the Morgans'," I commanded. "Touch that food and you're history."

Gregory frowned and turned to run upstairs. He bumped into Mom, who had just come into the dining room. She had a strange look on her face.

"Mom!" whined Gregory the Gross Out.

"Megan won't let me have anything to eat."

"Be quiet for a second, Gregory," said Mom. "I've got some bad news."

I froze—so did my friends. I could take almost any bad news—a tornado, a leprosy outbreak at school, World War III—anything except one thing.

"I just talked with Mrs. Morgan," Mom said. "She said that Jason is sick with a fever."

The words turned my blood icy cold. Shivers ran down my spine.

"So?" I asked, but I just knew what it meant.

Mom sighed. "I know you were expecting to have the house to yourselves tonight, girls. But we just can't take Gregory with us. He might catch what Jason has."

Jilly sighed.

Karen and Tammy looked at each other.

"We're doomed," was all I could say.

"Don't take it so hard, Megan," Mom said. "I'm sure Gregory won't do anything to ruin your party. He knows how important it is to you."

"We're doomed," I repeated.

"Gregory, you'll be good tonight, won't you? Dad asked. "I'll be very disappointed if I hear that you misbehaved."

Gregory nodded. But somehow it didn't make me feel much better. I looked at Gregory.

"I'm not happy about it either," he grumbled. "I don't want to stay here and listen to you talk about boys. I want to go mess around with Jason."

"If you want, we'll try to come home early," Mom said.

"It doesn't matter," I muttered. "Nothing matters now."

"Cheer up, dear," said Mom, kissing me good-bye. "I'm sure everything will be fine."

Then they left and we were alone—alone with Gregory the Gross Out. He had gone into the family room to watch TV. I looked at my friends' faces. They were trying to make the best of this bad situation, but I could tell they weren't any happier about it than I was. I mean, they had seen my brother in action. They knew what he could do!

For a few seconds no one said anything. Jilly was the first to speak. "When Courtney sees Gregory and finds out we lied to her, she'll hate us."

The rest of us nodded our heads.

"What are we going to do?" asked Tammy.

"Wait a minute!" I cried. "What if Courtney doesn't *see* Gregory?"

"What do you mean?" asked Karen.

"Come on," I said, motioning for them to follow me.

We all went into the family room where Gregory was watching TV. I turned down the sound and asked him, "Gregory, what would I have to do to make you disappear?"

Gregory just looked at me.

"I don't mean really disappear," I explained. "I just want you to vanish into your room and not come out until the party's over."

"I get it," whispered Tammy. "If Gregory stays in his room, she'll never know he's here."

"No way!" said Gregory as he crossed his arms. "What am I going to do in my room all that time?" he asked.

"Do what you always do. Play with Morty," I said. "Rearrange your dead bug collection."

"I already rearranged it," he said with a smirk.

"Please, Gregory," I begged. "I'll clean your room for a month if you do this for me."

"I don't want my room clean. I like it messy," he replied.

"Well, what do you want?" I asked in desperation. "We'll do anything."

Gregory grinned and I knew we were in trouble. "Since you cleaned up our house, there aren't any more bugs around," he began. "I want your friends to get bugs from their houses for me."

Jilly looked at Karen. Karen looked at Tammy. Tammy groaned. "You've got to do it," I said to them. "Courtney will be here any time."

Jilly sighed. "Okay," she said.

Tammy wrinkled her nose and said, "Okay."

Karen looked like she was about to gag. But she said, "Me too."

"And," continued Gregory, "Megan has to buy me ice cream after school every day for a week."

"Okay, okay," I agreed.

"And—" began Gregory.

"No! That's all!" I shouted. "Now get up-stairs and keep quiet!"

Gregory grinned. He grinned that grin that always makes me nervous. He turned and bounced up the stairs. We heard the door to his room slam. I shut the door to the dining room and we all walked into the living room.

"Whew," we all sighed. We collapsed on the couch together. But we had only rested for about half a minute before the doorbell rang.

"Are we all ready?" I asked.

Jilly nodded as she smoothed her dress with her hands. Karen gave me a thumbs-up. Tammy said, "We're as ready as we'll ever be."

I took a deep breath and headed for the front door.

Ten

"**H**I, Courtney," I said as I opened the door. "Come on in." Courtney smiled and stepped into the house.

"Hi everyone," Courtney said as she unbuttoned her jacket.

"Let me take that," I said as I reached for Courtney's jacket. "What a beautiful dress," Karen said to Courtney.

"Why don't we go into the living room and talk for a while," I suggested.

"Your house is very nice," Courtney said when we were sitting in the living room. "And it's spotless. How do you keep it so clean?"

"Uhh, it's...our maid," I said. "Our maid does a great job." I saw Jilly give Karen a funny look when I said that.

"Have your parents left for the neighbors' yet?" Courtney asked. "I'd like to say hi."

"They already left," I explained. "They probably won't be back until late."

Courtney shook her head. "That's one of the worst parts of being an only child, isn't it, Megan?" Courtney asked. "When your parents go out, you have to stay home all alone."

"Uhh, yeah, being alone is a real drag," I answered.

Just then we heard a loud thump up above us.

"What was that?" Courtney asked, looking up.

"What do you mean?" I asked. "I didn't hear anything."

But then we heard it again. It came from Gregory's room—naturally.

"Oh, that," I said with a laugh. "That's just...just the house settling. This is an old house."

After that rough start, things got better. I turned on the stereo to cover up any other sounds from upstairs. We started talking about boys in our class, and teachers at our school, and clothes and music and TV shows.

After a while, I had stopped worrying about the creature upstairs and got into having a good time. Courtney seemed to be having fun, too. I had forgotten all about how she seemed not to want to come to our party very much when I talked to her on the phone.

There was only one thing that was bugging me, way in the back of my mind. It was too quiet upstairs. I had expected Gregory to make a little bit of noise. But there was nothing. And when you can't hear or see Gregory the Gross Out, that's when you should worry!

"Hey," suggested Karen. "Let's have something to eat. I'm starved."

"Good idea," agreed Jilly as she got up from her chair. "Are you hungry, Courtney?"

"I sure am," answered Courtney.

"Let's go into the dining room," I said.

"Wait until you see all the food," Karen said.

"We had lots of fun fixing it and arranging

it on the table," added Tammy.

Karen opened the swinging door to the dining room and said, "Here we are. I hope you like it, Cour—"

Then she let out a screech.

"What's wrong?" I yelled.

"Let me see!" yelled Jilly.

Tammy pushed her way into the dining room, and the rest of us piled in after her.

I just about went into shock when I saw the table—the one we had worked so hard on. The trays of crackers were half empty. There were potato chips and olives everywhere, including floating in the punch. Popcorn was spilled on the floor. Sliced vegetables were sticking straight up in the dip. A trail of dip fingerprints led to the punch bowl. Grape punch was spilled all over Mom's good white tablecloth.

"What a mess!" said Courtney.

"Look!" said Karen. She pointed at a purple punch handprint on the side of the tablecloth. "Evidence."

"Who needs evidence?" I asked. Only one person could turn a beautiful party buffet into a disaster area!

"I'm really sorry about this," I said to Courtney. "I...I..."

My apology was interrupted by a noise. Coming from under the table, was a faint crunching sound.

"He's under the table!" shouted Jilly. "It sounds like he's eating potato chips. Let's get him!"

"Right!" said Karen.

"Get who?" asked Courtney. "Who's eating potato chips? What's going on?"

"Get ready," Jilly said. She and Karen were about to pull up the tablecloth. "You catch him when he comes out, Tammy! One...two...three!"

They flipped up the tablecloth. But it wasn't who they expected.

"YOW!" yelled Courtney, jumping back. "It's a mouse!"

A terrified Morty gave a squeak and bolted out from under the table. The poor thing ran right through Courtney's legs. He ran madly around the dining room and then took off for the living room.

"I'll get him," I hollered as I raced after the mouse into the living room. I watched him dive under the couch. "Help me move the couch," I shouted. "I've got him trapped behind it."

"Forget the mouse," called Jilly from the hallway. "Let's find the rat!"

"R-rat?" sputtered Courtney. "You mean you have mice *and* rats?"

"Just one rat," said Jilly. "And he's around here somewhere."

"Shh!" ordered Karen from the hall. "I think I hear something."

We all stood in the hallway, listening. Sure enough, we heard another crunching sound.

"I-is it a rat?" asked Courtney.

"It sure is," I said. I was so mad I could hardly think.

"AH-HA!" I shouted as I threw open the hall closet door. Sitting on the floor of the closet with a pile of food in his lap was My Brother the Gross Out—make that My Brother the Rat!

He just looked up at us and put his squirt gun in his mouth. He pulled the trigger and out shot a stream of grape punch. He had filled his squirt gun from our punch bowl! He had probably let Morty have a swim in it, for all I knew!

"Get out of there!" I screamed. Gregory stood up, dumping the food on his lap onto the floor.

"Isn't that the bug boy from school? The one with the spiked hair?" asked Courtney. "What's he doing in your closet, Megan?"

"Uhhh, what's he doing here...in my closet?" I repeated like an idiot. "Well, that's a good question. He...uhhh..."

"Megan is baby-sitting him again," said Jilly.

"Yeah," said Tammy. "That's why he's here."

I pulled Gregory out of the closet. "Give me that squirt gun," I ordered, trying to yank it out of his hand.

"No," yelled Gregory. We wrestled for a while. "It's mine!" I must have looked like a moron, playing tug-of-war over a squirt gun.

"You little mutant! You wrecked the table," I yelled.

"Let go," said Gregory as the gun pointed at me.

Just like in a movie when two guys are fighting over a gun, Gregory accidentally pulled the trigger. Squirt! Squirt! A stream of purple punch splashed right in my face.

"I'll just take this child upstairs right now. I'll be right back."

"But what about my mouse?" Gregory asked.

"I'll get him later," I growled. "Karen, why don't you get Courtney's present? Jilly, you can get the sandwiches that are left in the fridge."

"Megan," said Courtney. "I'm not—"

"No! No!" I said, cutting her off. "I'll be back in just a second." I grabbed Gregory by the hand and dragged him upstairs.

"But Courtney's present—" said Gregory.

"Don't talk to me!" I screeched. "You're ruining everything. If you make any more trouble tonight, I'll take you and Morty to the garbage dump and leave you there!"

"I'm not trying to make trouble," Gregory said. "It just happens."

"I'm not listening, so don't talk to me," I said as I pulled Gregory into my room. I wanted to change out of my white—make that *purple* and white—dress. When we walked into my room, I saw something on my bed.

It was the ballerina statue we'd bought for Courtney.

"What's that doing here?" I demanded. Gregory shrugged.

I looked him in the eye. "Did you take it out of the box?" I asked him.

He nodded.

"Why?"

"I needed another box for my bug collection," he said. "Why does Karen want my bugs anyway?"

117

"WHAT?!?!?"

"I tried to tell you, but you told me not to talk to you," he answered.

"Oh, no!" I tore out of my room, with Gregory following. I raced through the hall and flew down the stairs. But halfway down I stopped. Gregory bumped into me and practically knocked me over.

In the hallway below I could see Karen and Tammy huddled around Courtney. "Think of this gift as our way of welcoming you to Clover Hill," said Karen.

"DON'T OPEN IT!" I screamed. But I was too late. Courtney had lifted the lid.

"EE-YOOWWW!" she shreiked when she saw the dead bugs inside. She threw the box up into the air. Dead spiders, flies, beetles, water bugs, and moths went flying all over the hallway! Some of the bugs landed on the tray of sandwiches. A huge, shiny water bug landed on Karen's head.

"EEEK!" cried Jilly as she was showered with the dead bugs. She dropped the tray with

a crash and sandwiches tumbled all over the floor.

From halfway up the stairs, the four girls looked like they were doing some awful dance, jumping, hopping, and screaming their heads off.

"Gregory Evans! This is it!" I shouted. "You've embarrassed me for the very last time!"

Courtney looked up and saw us standing on the stairs. "Gregory Evans?" she repeated. "His last name is Evans?"

Karen, Jilly, and Tammy all got really quiet. I took a deep breath.

"Well, Courtney, I guess you were going to find out sooner or later," I said. "He's my brother, Gregory. I didn't want you to know I had such a gross little brother."

Courtney looked at Gregory. Then she looked at me. But the next thing she did was a total surprise.

Eleven

COURTNEY Collins Roth burst out laughing. She laughed and laughed. She bent over and held her stomach. She started to get tears in her eyes.

Jilly, Karen, and Tammy started to laugh, too. And even though I was boiling mad about what had happened, I started to giggle a little myself. I couldn't help it.

Gregory was the only one who wasn't laughing. "Hey!" he said. "What's so funny? Be careful where you step. I don't want any of my bugs to get squished!"

And you know what? That made us laugh even harder!

After we got the mess cleaned up, we got Morty out from under the couch. The poor thing looked pretty happy to be back in his aquarium cage and away from all the crazy stuff going on. All of us, including Gregory, sat down in the living room and gave Courtney our real welcoming present.

"You mean you're not mad?" Jilly asked Courtney.

"Mad?" Courtney asked. "Oh, no! This is the best party I've ever been to! I've never had so much fun in my life. When that mouse ran out from under the table I could have died laughing. But I just couldn't laugh because you all looked so serious. And Jilly, you should have seen the look on your face when those dead bugs landed on the sandwiches!"

"And you're not mad that I lied to you about my brother?" I asked.

She looked at me and smiled. "No, not at all," she answered.

Then I turned to Gregory, "I'm sorry I yelled at you, Gregory."

"That's okay, Megan." Then Gregory said, "Courtney, you're okay. For somebody who's rich, you're not stuck up at all!"

We all got quiet. Would Courtney get mad about what Gregory said?

But Courtney smiled. "Well, thanks, Gregory," she said. "I wish people wouldn't see me as a rich person. I wish they'd see me just as an ordinary kid."

I looked at Jilly. Courtney used the same words, ordinary kid, that we had used to describe ourselves. Courtney glanced around at the four of us.

"We really do like you because of who you are, not because you're rich," said Karen.

"I wasn't sure for a while there," Courtney said. "That's why I sort of didn't want to come tonight."

So that's why she acted a little strange when I invited her. It occurred to me that she'd probably had lots of people try to be friends with her just because she was rich.

Then I realized that I was one of those people. I felt ashamed of myself. Courtney was really a very nice person, and I was only looking at her as a rich person.

"You know what?" I asked, "I thought you wouldn't like me because I'm just an ordinary kid who likes to play basketball."

"I like basketball, too," said Courtney. "I was one of the best players at my boarding school."

"I thought I saw a basketball poster on your bedroom wall," said Karen.

"Let's all try to be on the same team this year," said Courtney.

"I also thought you might not want to be friends if you knew I had the grossest little brother in Clover Hill."

"Hey," said Gregory as he looked up from his bugs. "I never asked to be gross," he said, echoing what Courtney said about being rich.

That made us all laugh again.

"Actually," said Courtney, "I thought from the beginning that Gregory was kind of cute."

When she said that, something unbelievable happened. Gregory the Gross Out got embarrassed! He even blushed!

"The first time I saw him was when he was

trying to catch that fly in the lunchroom. And when he spiked his hair," said Courtney, "I thought to myself that a girl would never be lonely or bored with *that* boy for a brother!"

I had to laugh. "You're right about that part, Courtney," I said. "Things are definitely never boring with Gregory around."

"Well, if you ever want me to watch Gregory for an afternoon, you can bring him over any time," Courtney said. And I think she really meant it!

"Hey, you guys," said Karen. "I'm starving! Let's see if there's any food left. If it all got bugs on it, or ended up on the floor, maybe we can make some popcorn."

"Karen, you're always hungry," said Tammy.

"I'm hungry, too," said Courtney. She stood up and put her hand on Gregory's shoulder. "Come on, Gregory, let's go eat."

Suddenly I had an idea. As Gregory and Courtney walked out of the room, I whispered something to Jilly, Karen, and Tammy.

"It's the perfect revenge on Gregory the Gross Out!" whispered Jilly.

"We can pay him back for all the times he's embarrassed us!" added Tammy.

We walked up behind Gregory and Courtney. She looked back and saw us, but Gregory didn't. I put my finger to my lips so she wouldn't say anything. Then Jilly, Tammy, Karen, and I started singing as loud as we could:

Gregory's got a girlfriend!

Gregory's got a girlfriend!

Just as I thought he would, Gregory turned the color of a ripe tomato.

"Shut up!" he screamed.

Then Courtney did something that made Gregory the Gross Out turn even redder. It was the ultimate embarrassment.

She kissed him on the cheek!

"Oh gross!" shouted Gregory. He let out a terrible howl and ran out of the room. And the Fearsome Fivesome exploded into laughter!

About the Author

MICHAEL J. PELLOWSKI lives in New Jersey with his wife, Judith, and their four children, Morgan, Matthew, Melanie, and Martin. They also have two cats and a German shepherd. Before turning to writing, Michael was a professional football player and a high school teacher.

Michael is the author of more than 75 books for children, including the best-selling Double Trouble series about Sandi and Randi Daniels. He also works in TV production. His children's comedy show, *Fun Stop* was judged one of the best cable TV children's shows in the U.S.